Play With Me

BY MICHÈLE DUFRESNE

Pioneer Valley Educational Press, Inc.

The little puppy is looking
for a friend.
"Who will play with me?"
said the little puppy.

"Look, here is a friend.
Here is a friend for me!"

"Bella, will you play with me?"
said the little puppy.

Bella looked at the little puppy.
"No," said Bella.
"You are too little!"

"Look, here is a friend.
Here is a friend for me,"
said the little puppy.
"Rosie, will you play with me?"

Rosie looked at the little puppy.
"No," said Rosie.
"You are too little!"

"Who will play with me?"
said the little puppy.
"Oh, who will play with me?"

The little puppy cried.
He cried and cried and cried.

"OK," said Rosie.
"I will play with you."